The Day the Whale Came

WRITTEN BY **Eve Bunting**

ILLUSTRATED BY **Scott Menchin**

Harcourt Brace & Company

San Diego   New York   London

Library of Congress Cataloging-in-Publication Data
Bunting, Eve, 1928–
The day the whale came/Eve Bunting; illustrated by Scott Menchin.
p.   cm.
Summary: When Captain Pinkney brings the carcass of a dead whale to
Johnstown, Illinois, Tommy and his friend Ben go and pay to get a look.
ISBN 0-15-201456-X
[1. Whales—Fiction.   2. Friendship—Fiction.   3. Self-esteem—Fiction.]
I. Menchin, Scott, ill.   II. Title.
PZ7.B91527Dazi   1998
[Fic]—dc21   96-49816

First edition
A C E F D B
Printed in Singapore

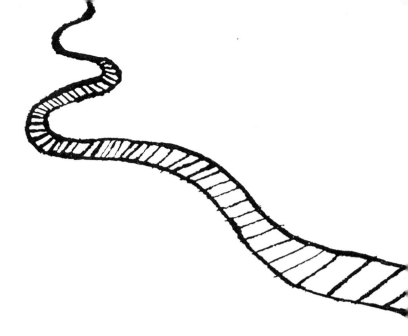

For Richard, my favorite son-in-law
—E. B.

For Mom, Dad, and Ivetta
—S. M.

My friend Ben and I walk along State Street. The maple trees flicker with swallows. Already it is hot.

We are going to see the whale. The whale is a real one, but the awful thing is, it's dead. In a way, I don't want to see it. But we don't often get a whale passing through Johnstown, Illinois. This may be my only chance.

"Tommy," Ben says, "look what I've brought." He slides his hand into the pocket of his overalls and when he brings it back out I see the enameled red of his penknife.

"I'm going to get me a whale souvenir," he says.

"What *kind* of souvenir?" I don't know what he means.

"A chunk of whale," he says.

My stomach lurches. "But . . . Captain Pinkney won't let you."

Captain Pinkney owns the dead whale. He's the one who's bringing it by train all the way across the country so people can see it. For educational purposes.

"I have a plan," Ben says.

I chew at my thumbnail. Ben's my friend. But sometimes I don't like the things he does. He gets mad if I say so, though. So usually I don't. I'm glad we're almost at the train station.

The platform is crowded.

Dr. Samuels is there in his Model A.

Mr. McPherson, our mayor, nods to us. "Hi, boys! Ready for the whale?"

I see Miss Dorothea Matthews, who runs the *Johnstown Gazette,* and there's a stranger with a fancy camera on a tripod. He has a black drape that he disappears under. Then he pops out again like a gopher from a hole.

"Here she comes!" somebody yells. The Johnstown Municipal Band that's lined up at the back of the platform starts playing "My Bonnie Lies over the Ocean" and the rest of us stand there, staring, waiting.

As the train gets closer I can see that it's not like an ordinary train. There are no passenger cars behind the engine, just a flatbed rolling car with a canvas roof. There is a crane at each end, and in the middle is lying this shapeless, gigantic black bulk.

"The whale," Ben breathes.

A man in green trousers and a green jacket is leaning out of the engine car, waving his cap. "Howdy, folks! Howdy!" he calls. Captain Pinkney.

The train shudders to a stop and the Captain holds up a hand, ordering the band to be quiet now, and they drift into silence.

"Good people of Johnstown, I am honored to be here," he shouts. Behind him I can see the great lump of the whale. There's ice around it, and water drips in a steady stream onto the track.

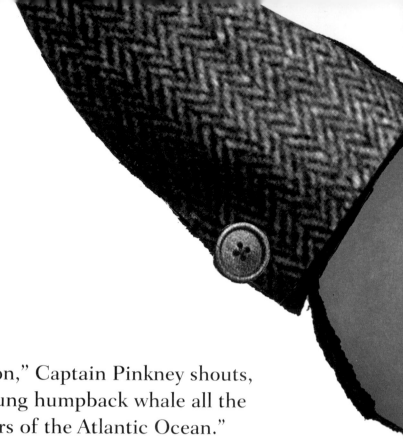

"For your appreciation," Captain Pinkney shouts, "I have brought this young humpback whale all the way from the cold waters of the Atlantic Ocean." He wipes his face with a red handkerchief. "Who knows why this great whale died, or how. But die he did." The Captain's voice rolls like a storm at sea and he jumps onto the platform. "Now, if you want a once-in-a-lifetime, close-up look at this marvelous creature, form a line in front of me. Ten cents for adults. A nickel for the kiddies."

The engineer gets down from the train and helps to push some wooden steps close to the whale's head.

I suddenly notice the smell. A fishy, rotten smell.

My dad and mom have arrived along with Ben's parents and they come over to us. Dad gives Ben and me each a nickel. Ben's holding his nose. "Peew, what a stinker!" he says.

"It's because he's been dead a while," Dad says.

Ben and I get in line. The adults are all letting the kids go first. I'm trying hard not to gag. From back here I can't see much except one of the whale's long flippers that's drooping down the side of the flatbed car.

I've read a lot about humpbacks. They're so graceful under water that divers say they're like great birds, their flippers beating like wings as they glide along. I swallow. I hope I'm going to be able to do this.

We're moving faster than I thought we would. We're almost there. Behind us, folks are dropping out of the line. I guess they can't stand the smell.

Ben nudges me, then opens his hand and shows me the penknife.

"I'll go first," he says. "You pretend to throw up when you're at the bottom of the steps and I'll cut me a piece of that flipper when nobody's looking."

"You couldn't," I say shakily. "It's tough as rubber."

Ahead of us the line's going faster than ever. Nobody's taking much time to look, that's for sure. Now Ben's climbing the steps. Captain Pinkney's keeping a close watch and Ben turns and gives me a meaningful look.

I act like I don't notice. I'm not going to pretend to be sick, even though I am, a bit.

Ben scowls at me as he comes back down. "You're some pal, Tommy," he whispers.

I go past him, climb the steps, and get my first look at the whale.

He's lying on a wood-and-canvas sling that's hooked to the cranes at each end. This isn't the whale the way it ever was. It has been too long from its oceans and too long from its life. My hands are shaking and I stuff them in my pockets. Everything is blurry and I don't know if it's because of the melting ice or because I'm puddling up with tears.

Now I am sick, no fooling.

Humpback families cross thousands of miles of ocean together. Mothers carry their babies on their backs. This one . . . this one . . .

"Hey, boy! You're taking too much time," Captain Pinkney bellows.

I come down and walk slowly along the length of the whale. The smell is so bad I can hardly breathe. The last of the grown folks are coming down the steps. The fireman is shoveling coal into the train furnace. Clouds of white vapor *sss* out of gaskets and pipes.

"Anybody else? Last chance to see the whale," Captain Pinkney shouts. "Got to get this show on the road."

I hate Captain Pinkney. Why didn't he leave the whale buried in its ocean?

The train starts to creak forward.

Captain Pinkney leans out of the engine car. "Thank you kindly, folks! Could be I'll be back someday with another fine educational attraction."

Some people wave and shout: "Bye, Captain Pinkney!"
I don't wave or shout. I hope he never comes back.
"Bye, whale," I whisper.
The band's playing "By the sea, by the sea, by the beautiful sea."
More than anything I want to go home.
And then Miss Dorothea Matthews says: "Look!"
The train has stopped about a half mile from town.
"What's wrong?" we shout, and we hurry, running and walking,
toward it.

"Doggone engine's broke down," Captain Pinkney shouts back.

We cluster below him in the dirt field. His face is all bulgy, and purple as prairie clover. "Engineer says it'll take a day to get it going. And I need fresh ice. I was fixing to get some in Stevenson." He fans himself with his hat. "Well. This whale's done for. This is as far as we go."

Everybody's shouting at once.

"What do you mean? What happens now?"

"Well, Jim here and I can't bury him ourselves. We'll need some help." He smoothes his mustache. " 'Course I can just dump him here, let him stink up the whole territory." He glances at the sky. "Looks like the wind's shifting in the direction of Johnstown, too."

We're all dumbfounded.

"It's your whale," somebody shouts.

"It's your town," Captain Pinkney says.

The mutters and the catcalls are getting ugly.

"How about we just bury you!" somebody else says, and everyone laughs except Captain Pinkney.

"Now, now," he says. "Nobody's fault, least of all mine."

The mayor takes charge. "We're caught in a bind here. I'm asking for volunteers to go home, get your shovels, and come back when it's cool. Let's pull together and give this poor creature a decent burial."

I like the way our mayor says that. If he's still around when I'm older I'll definitely vote for him.

Seems the whole town's willing to pull together. It's not every night we get to bury a whale.

An early moon is sailing high when we start digging the trench that needs to be as long as the whale's flatcar.

The photographer is falling all over himself getting pictures and Miss Dorothea Matthews is scribbling notes like crazy.

It takes all that night and well into the morning before we get finished. At the end we're working in shifts, sleeping in the backs of wagons, digging and sleeping. But we get it done.

The Captain stands on top of the engine car and gives directions, then he and the train man crank up the cranes. The whale cradle swings out and hangs over the trench. "Let's tip him in," the Captain says.

The black mass slides off and it seems the whole earth shudders.

The whale has gone in on his side and his right flipper has somehow folded itself across his body. Sometimes humpbacks fold their flippers like that when they're resting in the ocean. Remembering that makes me feel better.

Then I see Ben opening his penknife. Does he think he can reach down to cut the whale? He's going to try.

I fling myself at him and the knife flies out of his hand. I grab it and throw it as far as I can. We're rolling over and over in the dirt.

"You're nuts," Ben says. "You've gone and lost my knife. The whale's stone-cold dead. Who cares about him?"

I hold Ben down and stare into his face. "I do," I say.

Dad puts his arm around my shoulders, and Ben's mom grabs the back of his neck and gives him a little shake. He glares at me, but his glare doesn't scare me the way it usually does.

I help the others scoop black Illinois dirt over our dead humpback. We don't put up a marker or anything, but we won't forget the whale and the day he came to Johnstown.

That winter I walk out to the place where we buried him. Comber Stanislawski comes with me. He's my best friend now. He was there the night we buried the whale and he says I was right not to let Ben cut him, even if he was dead. I like Comber a lot. I think Ben was only my friend because we live next door and because I let him boss me around. After the whale, he told me I owed him fifty cents for a new penknife, and I told him to go take a long jump off a short pier. There aren't any piers close by but I think he got the message. It's funny, after I stuck up for the whale it wasn't that hard to stick up for myself.

I talked to my mom about it. She says sticking up for something you believe in and sticking up for yourself are the same thing.

In the spring I go alone to the whale place and I can't believe
what I see. Above where the whale is buried there's a great
splash of color. Hundreds and hundreds of wildflowers, pink
and red and yellow and blue, are growing so thickly together
they look like a carpet. And the carpet is the shape of the whale
resting on its side.

Moss pinks, cow parsnips, bluebells . . . I know the names of some of the flowers. A sprinkling of them appear on the ground around here. But I've never seen them clumped like this.

I can hardly breathe. The whale didn't know land. But its death made this land rich. Once the whale had been beautiful. It is beautiful again.

I look at it till it shimmers in front of my eyes, and it seems as if the humpback is swimming, swimming, a flower whale gliding into the sun.

The illustrations in this book were done in pen and ink in collage.
The display type was hand-lettered by the illustrator.
The text type was set in Fairfield Medium.
Color separations by Bright Arts, Ltd., Singapore
Printed and bound by Tien Wah Press, Singapore
This book was printed on totally chlorine-free Nymolla Matte Art paper.
Production supervision by Stanley Redfern
Designed by Lydia D'moch

"How do you know?" asked the boy.

"Because I belong in her heart," said Suki,
turning to wave goodbye.

"Remember, I'm coming back for you at three,"
said Suki's mother, kissing her.

"I know you are," said Suki as the boy pulled her
away.

On Monday, when Suki and her mother got to
Mrs. Clara's Child Care Center, some of the children
were already there. The boy with red hair ran up and
grabbed Suki's hand.

"Come on," he said. "Play supermarket with us.
You can be a customer."

"No," said Suki.

And Suki's mother put the two pieces of the heart back together.

"There," said her mother. "You're back where you belong."

"Will I always belong there?" asked Suki.

"Always," said her mother, giving Suki a big hug.

"Let's pretend this is my heart," said her mother.
"Because I love you, you have a special place in it."
She wrote Suki's name in the heart. "When I leave
you at Mrs. Clara's on Monday, I'll leave a part of my
heart, too." And she tore Suki's name from the heart.
"I can't let Mrs. Clara have a part of my heart very
long, can I?"

"Poor Lulu," said Suki's mother. "Her head was filled with worry that you would not come back for her. She couldn't think of anything else!"

"Silly Lulu," said Suki. "I won't act like her when you leave me with Mrs. Clara, will I?"

"Of course you won't," said her mother as she finished making a big red heart. "You know I'll come back for you every day at three o'clock."

"I guess so," said Suki. She looked at the heart for a long time. "But how do I know you'll come back for me?" she asked.

"Silly Lulu," said Suki, picking up Lulu Bear. "You knew I had other things to do."

Suki's mother got out a pair of scissors and some red paper. "Did Lulu ever play with the other bears?" she asked as she started to make something.

"No," said Suki. "No matter what Brown Bear or the other bears did, Lulu just sat in a chair by herself. And when everyone went outside to play, she stood by the fence and stared and stared."

"I'd never, ever forget Lulu!" cried Suki.

"Of course you wouldn't," said her mother.

"At snack time, Lulu wouldn't sit at the table with the other bears," said Suki. "So Brown Bear set a little table in front of her with graham crackers and milk. You know that's her favorite snack. And she wouldn't even look at it."

"Poor Lulu," said her mother. "Maybe she was waiting to share with you like she always does."

Her mother began to brush Suki's hair. "Did Lulu Bear stop crying after you left?"

"After a while," said Suki. "A panda bear tried to get Lulu to help him build a tower with blocks. And a koala bear wanted her to draw a picture. But Lulu ran to the window, shoved it open, and called me."

"Poor Lulu," said her mother. "Maybe she thought you'd forgotten where you left her."

"Oh," said her mother.

"And she was very upset," said Suki.

"What did she do?" asked her mother.

"She cried when I started to leave," said Suki. "I told her I would be back for her. But she just kept on crying."

"Poor Suki," said her mother, hugging her. "What did you do?"

"I hurried away before I started to cry, too," said Suki.

"That was hard to do, wasn't it?" asked her mother.

"Yes," said Suki.

When she went to bed, she tossed and turned and turned and tossed in her sleep.

The next morning, her mother found the sheets and blankets and Suki and Lulu Bear all bunched together in a tangled bundle.

"I dreamed that I took Lulu Bear to Brown Bear's School for Teddies," said Suki as her mother freed her from the twisted bedclothes.

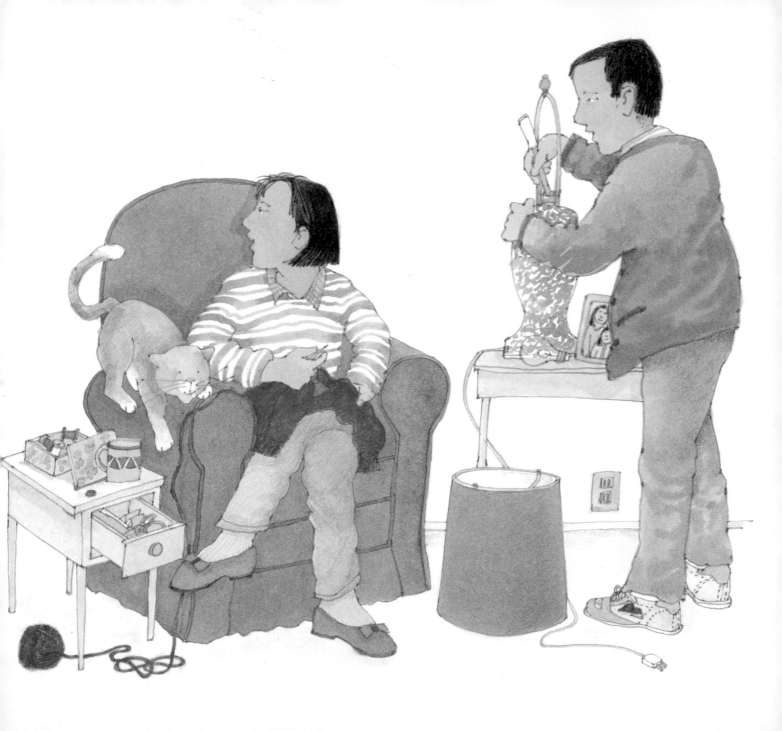

That night after dinner, Suki's mother and father talked with her about the Child Care Center.

"Wouldn't it be nice to learn how to write your name?" asked her mother.

"Just think of all the new friends you'll have to play with," said her father.

"Anyway," said her mother, "we'd like you to give it a try."

Suki was very quiet.

When the boys and girls were getting ready for
their rest time, Suki and her mother got ready to leave.
  "I hope I'll see you soon," Mrs. Clara told Suki.
Suki didn't say anything.

"Snack time," announced Mrs. Clara. "Won't you join us?" she asked Suki as a boy with red hair offered her a carton of milk.

Suki shook her head. Then she watched the children enjoy their milk and graham crackers.

While Mrs. Clara talked with her mother, Suki and Lulu Bear peeked from behind her. They watched one girl paint a picture while another girl helped a boy with his train.

A few minutes later, Suki and her mother wandered over to see what some boys and girls were building with blocks. Then they went to the window and looked at the children playing on swings and slides.

The next day Suki's mother took her to visit Mrs. Clara's Child Care Center. And Suki took Lulu Bear.

"Will I like school?" asked Suki.

"I hope so," said her mother. "And how happy I'll be, knowing you're busy at school while I'm working with Daddy."

It was Suki's fourth birthday.

After everyone had watched Suki open her
presents, her father said, "Sometimes four-year-olds
go to school."

"Why?" asked Suki.

"Wouldn't you like to learn about numbers and
letters?" asked Suki's grandmother.

"Yes," said Suki, "but what would Mommy do
while I was at school?"

"Daddy needs my help in his office," said Suki's
mother.

"Oh," said Suki.

Especially For

Elayne
Falk
A.T.

My Mom

R.K.

Library of Congress Cataloging-in-Publication Data

Tompert, Ann.
Will you come back for me?
SUMMARY: Four-year old Suki is worried about being left in day care
for the first time until her mother reassures her that she loves her
and will always return for her.
[1. Day-care centers — Fiction.   2. Fear — Fiction.
3. Parent and child — Fiction.]   I. Kramer, Robin, ill.   II. Title
PZ7.T598Wi   1988   [E]   87-37258
ISBN 0-8075-9112-2 (lib. bdg.)
ISBN 0-8075-9113-0 (pbk.)

Will You Come Back for Me?

Ann Tompert *pictures by* Robin Kramer

ALBERT WHITMAN & COMPANY

GROVE, ILLINOIS

Will You Come Back for Me?

Not only did they claim that their denim was the best in the world, but that their jeans and boots and hats had a certain extra quality to them. They said that their exclusive designs were invisible to anyone who was not fit for the job he or she held, or who was otherwise stupid or foolish.

"Whoa!" said the Emperor. "Let me get this straight. You're telling me that if I wear your exclusive clothes, I'll know which people in my company are not qualified for their position? And I'll be able to pick out the losers from the movers and shakers?"

"Sure as we're sitting here, sir!"

"Well then, I'll place a large order. And I'll need it ASAP!"

The so-called tailors smiled at each other. "Well, sir, since we can already tell you're such a good customer, we'll make you this special one-time offer. We wouldn't do this for just anybody, but since you're the Emperor, have we got a deal for you!"

The Emperor gave the two swindlers a lot of money in advance so they could start working right away. They set up shop in an old warehouse, and pretended to be fashioning jeans out of the best quality denim and sewing beautiful silk shirts, but really they were doing a whole lot of nothing.

At the outset, they had asked for a pile of gold for belt buckles, a big bag of rhinestones to decorate the hand-tailored jackets, and some very pricey silver thread to stitch on the jeans. But they put all of that into their own pockets while they worked away at empty sewing machines until the wee hours of the morning.

A couple of weeks went by. *Hmmm. . .
I wonder how those tailors are getting on with
my new wardrobe*, thought the Emperor. He
felt a little funny when he remembered how
they'd said that anyone who was stupid or unfit
for their job wouldn't be able to see the clothes.
He wasn't worried for himself, mind you, but
he thought he'd send somebody else to check
it out for him first.

So the Emperor sent his chief advisor to pay a visit to the two swindlers, who were sitting behind empty sewing machines.

Good heavens! thought the Emperor's chief advisor, opening his eyes wide. *I don't see a thing!* But he wasn't about to let on.

The two swindlers asked him if he wouldn't mind coming closer.

"Isn't this exquisite stitching on these jeans?" asked one.

"Don't you just love the etching on this here gold belt buckle?" asked the other.

While they were talking they pointed to the empty sewing machine. The Emperor's chief advisor kept on staring, but he couldn't see anything, because of course there wasn't anything there.

Gracious me, he thought to himself. *Could I be one of the fools they're talking about? Am I unfit for my job? Will I get fired? There's no way I can tell anyone that I couldn't see the clothes!*

"Well, sir, what do you think?" asked the tailor who was pretending to stitch the denim jeans.

"Oh, they're beautiful. Really! And the belt, it's a masterpiece!"

Then the two swindlers asked for more money, for top-grain leather for boots, and fine wool felt for hats, and more silk, and silver and gold thread, saying they needed all that to complete the Emperor's wardrobe. But again they put the money in their own pockets, and just went on working at their empty sewing machines.

Now the Emperor decided he wanted to see his
new wardrobe while it was still being made.

So, along with his entourage, he paid a visit to the imposters, who were working as hard as ever at the empty machines.

"It's fabulous!" said the Emperor's advisors. "Look at the hand-tooled leather and beautiful stitching!" They pointed to the empty machines, because they thought for sure everybody else could see the stuff.

Good Lord! thought the Emperor. *Why, I don't see the first thing they're talking about!*

Am I the biggest fool of all? Will everyone think I'm not qualified to be Emperor? Why, I'll be the laughingstock of the entire city. Oh, what a mess I'm in!

The Emperor was filled with doubt, but out loud all he said was, "This is a work of art! The best in the entire world!" No one was going to get him to admit that he, of all people, couldn't see anything.

His entire entourage looked and stared, but not a one of them could see the clothes. But do you think any of them would admit it either?

Instead they all agreed that this was the greatest stuff they'd ever laid eyes on.

"Awesome!" "Positively inspired!" "Brilliant!" they all exclaimed. They even advised the Emperor to wear one of his new outfits to a Big Event that was about to take place.

So the two imposters pretended to take the jeans and jacket out of the sewing machines. They held them in the air and trimmed the threads with big old scissors, and polished the boots and rhinestones with a special cloth.

Finally they said, "Announcement, announcement!
The Emperor's new wardrobe is ready!"

"Here are your jeans, Emperor, and your silk shirt and sparkly jacket. And your custom-made boots and hand-tooled leather belt with the gold belt buckle."

"And no outfit would be complete without your own personal cowboy hat! It's all light as a feather, too. You might think you're not wearing a thing, but that's part of the beauty of our exclusive designs!"

"Wow!" "Whoa!" "Amazing!" said the entourage, but they couldn't see anything, of course. The two tailors asked the Emperor to take off his clothes so they could help him fit into his new outfit. So the Emperor did just that and stood in front of a big mirror while the swindlers pretended to give him one piece after another of his fancy new wardrobe.

The Emperor turned around and around, admiring himself in the mirror, while everybody oohed and aahed.

"Sir, your horse is waiting to take you to the Big Event, whenever you're ready."

"Oh, I'm ready all right, to lead the parade in my new duds!" said the Emperor, looking in the mirror one more time.

When the Emperor's horse arrived at the Big Event, the streets were lined with folks waiting to catch a glimpse of the Emperor's new clothes. As the Emperor approached, he smiled and waved.

The crowd cheered. "Love the new clothes, Emperor!" "Yeah, great look!" None of the Emperor's clothes had ever been this popular before. Not a soul would let on that they couldn't actually see the clothes, because nobody wanted to look foolish, stupid, or worse!

Then the Emperor climbed down off his horse.

"The Emperor ain't wearing no clothes at all!" said a little boy in the crowd.

"Listen to my innocent son," said the little boy's daddy, and one by one everybody started whispering, "The Emperor's not wearing any clothes!"

One man yelled to his wife, "Don't look, Ethel!" But it was too late—she saw the Emperor wearing nothing but his birthday suit.

The Emperor, who knew it was all too true, tried his best to appear dignified. But he picked up the pace of the parade while the crowd yelled, "He's naked as a jaybird!"

And the Emperor just kept on running!

This just goes to show you that sometimes it takes the eyes of a child to see the truth for what it really is.